In memory of Opus for Russ, Palmer, Milo and the doctors and staff at N.E.V.O.G. (AHK)

To Steve, my husband, for all his love and support. (SK)

Text © 2008 by Alice Howard Koesterich
Illustrations © Sara Kahn

Typeset in Filosofia and CafeMimi
The illustrations in this book were rendered in acrylics, gouache, and watercolor pencil.
Manufactured in China by Regal Printing

Library of Congress Cataloging has cataloged the Foggy Dog Edition as: 2007909934

foggydog books

www.opusandtheredchair.com

Opus and the Red Chair

By Alice Howard Koesterich

Illustrated by Sara Kahn

Foggy Dog Books · San Francisco

My name is Opus and I've been a
Boston dog as long as I can remember.

Three humans live with me in my house:
Ben, Lily, and a kid named Petey.

Every day Lily and Petey walk me to the Boston Commons to play with my pals. I love chasing my ball and rolling in the grass to look at the world *upside down*.

I'm **always** hungry after playing
in the park, so we stop by to visit my
best friend Ken at the pet store.

Ken gives me lots of *yummy* treats. Sometimes, when Ken isn't looking, I grab a few more.

I think he sees me, but he *pretends* he doesn't.

I *love* those treats but pizza is my *favorite* food. When we walk by the pizzeria, I like to just sit and smell the *wonderful* pizzas cooking. I look at the people with my big brown eyes hoping they will give me their *crusts!*

Lily struggles to pull me away from the pizzeria. It's a game for us each day. I try not to budge, while she tries to get me to move.

Eventually I let her win and we walk home. One day someone *will* give me a *whole pizza slice!*

When I get home, **nothing** makes me happier than sleeping in my *comfy red chair* next to the window over looking the street.

My red chair hugs my body and makes me feel *better* when I'm sick or scared of thunderstorms.

I *love* my life in Boston, so one day
when two large men arrive at our house
and start packing my family's things,
I begin to *worry*.

I watch clothes, toys, and plates disappear into large boxes. Even my own toys are getting packed up. Why are those toys sealed up in brown boxes?

Where are they going?

And just where do they think they are going with *my red chair?*

Soon the house is **completely** empty.
The floors are so cold and hard.
Is my family going to leave me alone?

I want to nap in my red chair, but
it's not here. Maybe if I sit in the spot
where the chair **used to be** it will
come back.

A taxi pulls up in front of our house and my family helps me get in the back seat.

I'm *so happy* to be going with them.

The window is rolled down, and the wind blows my fur.
The smell of the Charles River reminds me of warm
summer days spashing in the water and chasing after ducks.

When the taxi stops, we are at the airport.
The noises are loud and people are everywhere.
I'm scared. And I don't see any other dogs.

Lily gives me a big hug and puts my *favorite* Teddy bear in my mouth to cheer me up.

A nice man in a uniform helps me get into a huge crate with holes.
Being in this crate makes me feel *better*. It makes Teddy feel *better* too.

I look out and watch my family and all the busy people at the airport.
I wonder if anyone will give me a **treat**?

Soon I am on an airplane. It is very quiet. I am the only dog in a room filled with luggage. The humming of the engines makes me sleepy so I take a nice *long nap*.

I hold Teddy and **dream** of curling up in my **red chair** after a walk, eating pizza, and chasing my ball.

I wake up to hear familiar voices.
Ben opens the crate door
and Teddy and I almost knock him
over when we jump out.

I run to Lily and Petey and lick their faces.
I bark and bark and bark.
I am so happy to see them.

We get into another taxi. This time the sights and sounds outside the window are **so different!**

Palm trees are blowing in the wind and fog horns are bellowing out on the bay.

Lily and Ben talk to Petey about our new home. I am **excited** but a little nervous too.

On the way we pass some dogs playing in the park.

I'm *glad* to see there are dogs here.

We drive up to a house and my family opens the door and I run up the stairs.

And what do I see?

It's my comfy red chair!

I run to my chair and curl up with Teddy and fall fast asleep. Now I have new dog friends that I play with every day. And instead of playing at the Boston Commons, I run on the beach, roll in the grass, and sleep in my comfy red chair, in my new home in California.